This Ladybird book
belongs to

_____

A catalogue record for this book is available
from the British Library

Published by Ladybird Books Ltd
A subsidiary of the Penguin Group
A Pearson Company
© LADYBIRD BOOKS LTD MCMXCVII

Forgetful
Little
Fireman

by Alan MacDonald
illustrated by Philip Hopman

Little Fireman Hugh of Fire Crew Number Two was having his breakfast. He was just pouring milk on his cornflakes when the fire station bell rang. *Ring a ding ding! Ring a ding ding!*

The fire chief stuck his head round the door.

"Hurry! Hurry!" he called. "We're needed at Polly's pet shop. The animals have got out and Polly can't find them."

There was no time to lose. Fire Crew Number Two sprang into action.

Little Fireman Hugh was first to slide down the pole. He jumped onto the red engine. But he was in such a hurry he'd forgotten something.

"Wait!" said the chief. "You can't go out in your socks!"

"Oh gadzooks!" cried Hugh. "I've forgotten my boots."

He rushed back upstairs. He pulled on his boots and slid down the pole.

"Hurry! Hurry!" called the chief. "We've got to rescue Polly's pets."

Little Fireman Hugh jumped on and started the red engine.

"Wait!" said the chief. "You can't go without your helmet!"

"Look at that!" cried Hugh. "I've forgotten my hat!"

Fireman Hugh flew back upstairs. He snatched his helmet and slid down the pole.

"Hurry! Hurry!" called the chief. "We've got to rescue Polly's pets."

Little Fireman Hugh jumped into the driver's seat again.

This time he made sure that he'd got everything. "Got my helmet, got my boots, got my jacket. Let's go!"

He started the engine and drove off.

"Wait! Wait!" called the chief. "You've left ME behind!"

"Oh, good grief!" cried Hugh. "I've forgotten the chief!"

He looked back and saw the chief puffing down the road after them.

Come back!

Hugh stopped the fire engine and the chief jumped on.

"*Now* let's go!" cried the chief. "We've got to rescue Polly's pets."

Little Fireman Hugh drove the engine fast through the streets.

"WEE! WOO! Let me through!" went the siren.

Cars stopped to let the fire engine go by. Fire Crew Number Two held on tight as they swung round corners and raced through the traffic.

At last they arrived at Polly's pet shop. Polly was waiting at the door.

"Thank goodness you're here," she said. "There was a storm last night and all the animals escaped from the pet shop. I've looked everywhere but I can't find them. What will I do if they don't come back?"

"Don't worry, Polly," said the chief. "They can't have gone far. Fire Crew Number Two will find them."

Fire Crew Number Two split up to search for Polly's pets.

Little Fireman Hugh looked in Polly's garden. He looked in the flower beds, he looked under bushes, he looked in the shed – but he didn't find any pets.

Then a voice squawked, "Who's a clever boy then?"

Fireman Hugh looked up.

"Bring the ladder," he called.
"There's a parrot in the pear tree."

Fireman Hugh climbed the ladder
and the parrot hopped onto his
shoulder.

Soon it was safely back in its cage.

Then Hugh had a look in Polly's house.

He looked in the cupboards, he looked up the chimney, he looked under the table – but he couldn't find any pets.

Then he heard a hissing sound coming from the kitchen...

"Help!" said Fireman Hugh.
"There's a snake in the sink!"

Carefully Fireman Hugh carried
the snake back to Polly. Soon it
was safely back in its box.

Next he went upstairs to look in the bedroom.

He looked behind the curtains, he looked in the wardrobe, he looked under the bed – but he didn't find any pets.

Then he heard snoring coming from under the bedcovers…

"Well, I never!" said Hugh. "Three puppies sharing a pillow!"

Soon the puppies were back in the shop along with all the other pets.

"There you are," smiled the chief. "I said they hadn't gone far."

"Thanks so much for finding my pets," said Polly. "The only one still missing is Tilda the tortoise. I do hope she isn't lost."

"That reminds me," said Hugh, "I do beg your pardon. I think I left my helmet out in your garden."

Fire Crew Number Two all laughed. Trust Fireman Hugh to have forgotten something!

But when they all went out in the garden they saw something very strange. Hugh's helmet was crawling off down the path by itself...

Hugh picked it up. Underneath was Tilda the tortoise.

"Oh, how clever, you've found Tilda!" said Polly and gave Hugh a big kiss. Fireman Hugh blushed as red as his engine.

Sometimes he didn't mind being a little fireman who was a little forgetful.